MÄK
YOUR MARK

Farshore

First published in Great Britain 2022 by Farshore
An imprint of HarperCollins*Publishers*
1 London Bridge Street, London SE1 9GF
www.farshore.co.uk

HarperCollins*Publishers*
1st Floor, Watermarque Building, Ringsend Road
Dublin 4, Ireland

Licensed by:

Hasbro

MY LITTLE PONY and HASBRO and all related trademarks and
logos are trademarks of Hasbro, Inc. ©2022 Hasbro.

ISBN 978 0 0085 3235 2
Printed in Great Britain by Bell and Bain Ltd, Glasgow
001

A CIP catalogue record for this title is available from the British Library.

MEET THE MANE 5

SUNNY STARSCOUT

Sunny is a courageous Earth Pony who always stands up for what she believes in.

HITCH TRAILBLAZER

Hitch is the Sheriff of Maretime Bay. He is a kind-hearted Earth Pony with a natural talent for caring for animals.

IZZY MOONBOW

Izzy is a creative Unicorn who enjoys crafting and inventing new things.

PIPP PETALS

Princess Pipp is a royal Pegasus Pony and superstar. She loves singing on stage for all her fans.

ZIPP STORM

Princess Zipp is an athletic Pegasus Pony who much prefers going on adventures to her royal duties.

A lot had changed in Equestria since Sunny and her friends had reunited the Unity Crystals.

The Earth Ponies, Unicorns and Pegasi now shared the land together and magic had returned once more.

And best of all, Sunny had her best pony friends by her side.

One day Sunny had a big announcement for the ponies of Maretime Bay. Sunny smiled into the camera of Pipp's phone as she recorded a video message.

"Hey everypony! Come to our Maretime Bay Day celebration. This year **ALL** ponykinds are welcome. It's going to be a blast!"

Sunny and her friends couldn't wait for the big day!

But not all the Earth Ponies were pleased that the magical Pegasi and Unicorns were invited that year.

One Earth Pony named Posey angrily marched over and huffed, "Well, I wish magic had never come back, and I'm not the only pony around here who thinks so! We want Maretime Bay Day to be magic-free!"

"You Pegasi are always flying too fast and you Unicorns use your magic for everything – I almost got hit in the head by a bag of floating apples at the market yesterday!" she continued, "Magic is not safe, at least not for the rest of us ponies who don't have it!"

Posey turned up her nose and marched off in a huff. But Sunny was not put out – she was determined to prove to all the ponies that magic is **AWESOME**.

The next day, Sheriff Hitch got an emergency call from the beach. When he arrived, a crowd of ponies were arguing with the remains of a flattened sandcastle between them. An Earth Pony was accusing a Unicorn of ruining it on purpose.

The Unicorn cried, "I'm telling you – it was an accident. I was carrying the umbrella and then my magic just stopped working."

But the ponies could not agree. Hitch had to get the ponies to stop arguing.

Meanwhile, magical mishaps had been happening all over Maretime Bay. And the more the ponies argued, the worse it got.

Zipp had noticed her flying powers were glitching. She watched in dismay as a crowd of ponies quarrelled on the beach.

The more ponies fought, the worse the weather got, too. As the days went on, the sky got darker with ominous flashes of lightning. And back at the Crytal Brighthouse, the Unity Crystals were giving off sparks.

Zipp was worried. Something weird was going on ...

After some investigating, Zipp realised what was happening and rushed back to the Crystal Brighthouse to tell the others.

Catching her breath, she said, "I think I know why magic is glitching. When ponies aren't treating each other with **KiNDNESS**, the magic becomes unstable."

Together they came up with a plan. They decided that Maretime Bay Day was the perfect opportunity to bring all the ponies together and help them be friends.

Maretime Bay Day finally arrived. The town was buzzing with excitement and the streets were covered with decorations.

Sunny trotted on to the main stage to announce that the Maretime Bay Day concert was about to begin.

"Everypony please welcome to the stage Princess Pipp Petals, to sing the **BRAND NEW** Maretime Bay Day song!"

But before Pipp could begin to sing, Posey and some of the other Earth Ponies started shouting.

"We want to hear the **REAL** Maretime Bay Day song, sung by an Earth Pony!"

They would not be persuaded to give Pipp a chance.

As the crowd angrily shouted and booed, there was a loud crash of thunder and back at the Crystal Brighthouse, the Unity Crystals were beginning to crack.

The wind picked up, tearing apart all the decorations. Then a bolt of lightning struck a tree and the ground split open, making a **BiG BLACk HOLE**!

All the Unicorns' glowing horns flickered out and the Pegasi could no longer fly.

"Oh no! the magic is dying!" shouted Sunny.

The ponies in the crowd began to scream and run away – but the Earth Ponies' hooves were stuck to the ground and they couldn't move. They were **TRAPPED**!

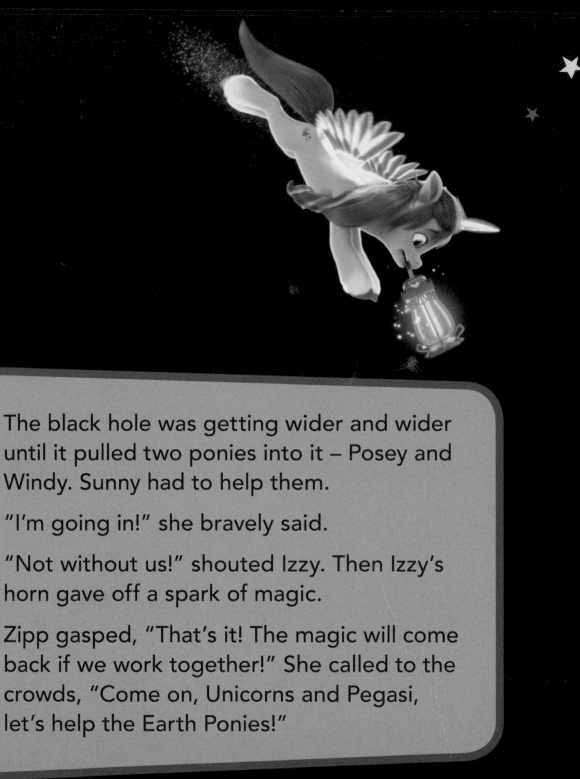

The black hole was getting wider and wider until it pulled two ponies into it – Posey and Windy. Sunny had to help them.

"I'm going in!" she bravely said.

"Not without us!" shouted Izzy. Then Izzy's horn gave off a spark of magic.

Zipp gasped, "That's it! The magic will come back if we work together!" She called to the crowds, "Come on, Unicorns and Pegasi, let's help the Earth Ponies!"

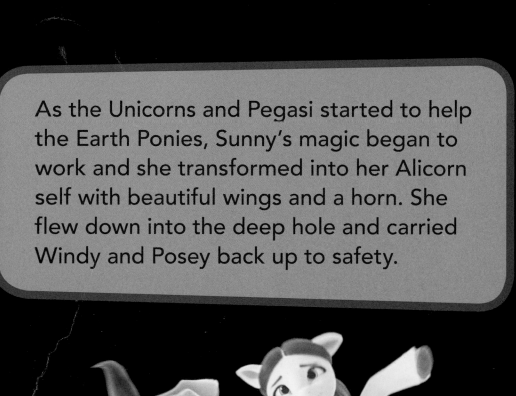

As the Unicorns and Pegasi started to help the Earth Ponies, Sunny's magic began to work and she transformed into her Alicorn self with beautiful wings and a horn. She flew down into the deep hole and carried Windy and Posey back up to safety.

As all the ponies helped each other, an **EPIC** magic blast burst from the black hole.

The Earth Ponies' hooves were released from the ground, and they soon discovered that they now had amazing new magical powers.

With the magic that glowed from their hooves, the Earth Ponies fixed the broken tree and sealed up the cracks in the ground.

Zipp was amazed. She said, "When we work together, maybe we can invent new magic!"

With the black hole closed up, soon harmony was restored to the land.

Later that day, Posey trotted over to the Mane 5, looking embarrassed.

"Hey everypony," she said, "I'm really sorry for the way I acted."

She was thankful that they had saved her life and now she understood that magic wasn't something to be scared of.

The Mane 5 were happier than ever now that everyone was friends and the magic had been restored.

What's more, Hitch had been so impressed with Zipp's investigation skills that he had made her a detective! Zipp was filled with pride.

With a smile on her face, Sunny said, "No matter what lies ahead, we'll face it **TOGETHER**."